The Annual Royal Bake-Off

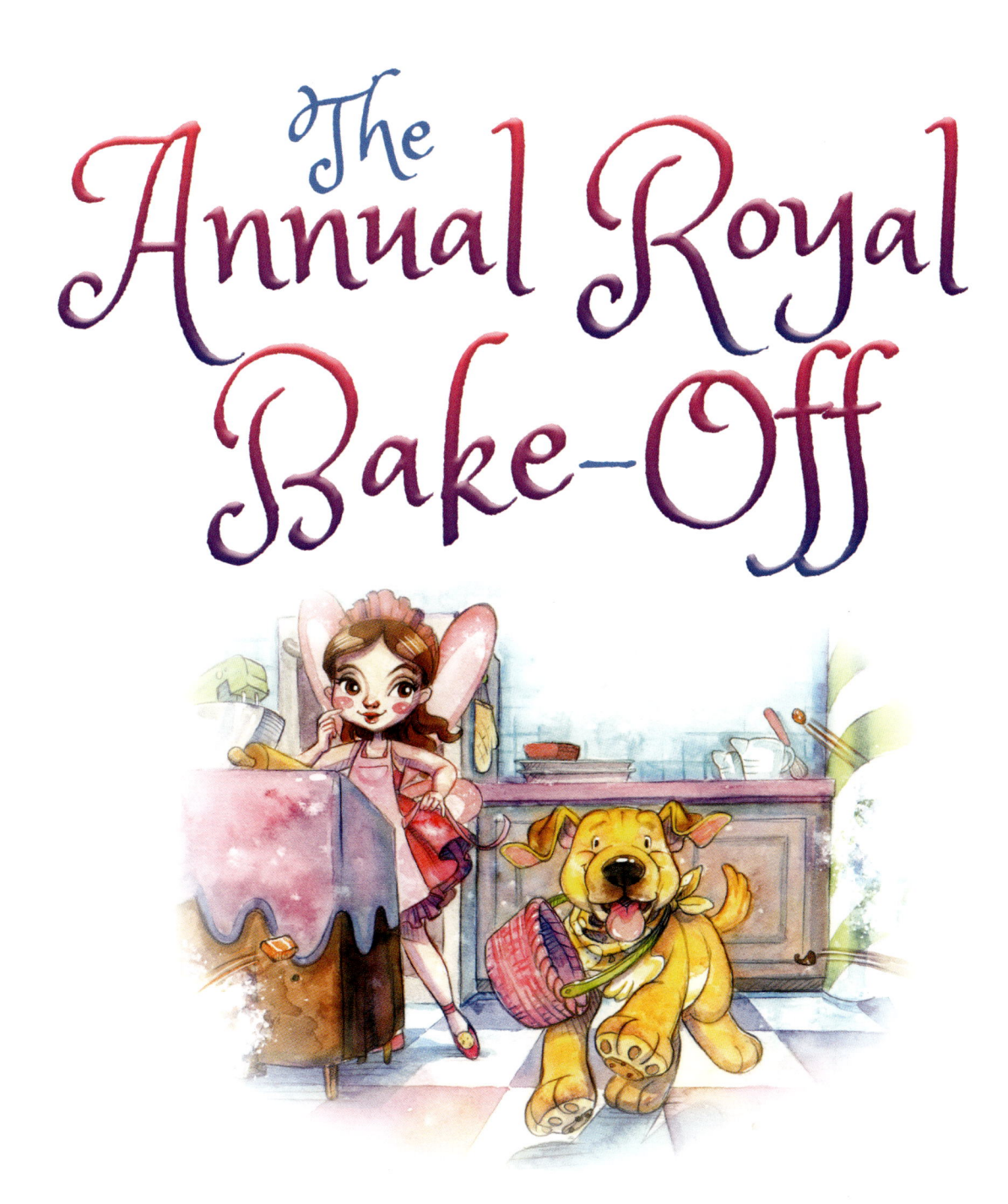

Written by Jordan and Monica Mitidieri Illustrated by Anne Zimanski

Copyright © 2020 by Jordan and Monica Mitidieri.

All rights reserved. This book or any portion thereof may not be reproduced or used in any manner whatsoever without the express written permission of the publisher except for the use of brief quotations in a book review.

First Printing, 2020

ISBN: 978-1-7346527-0-3

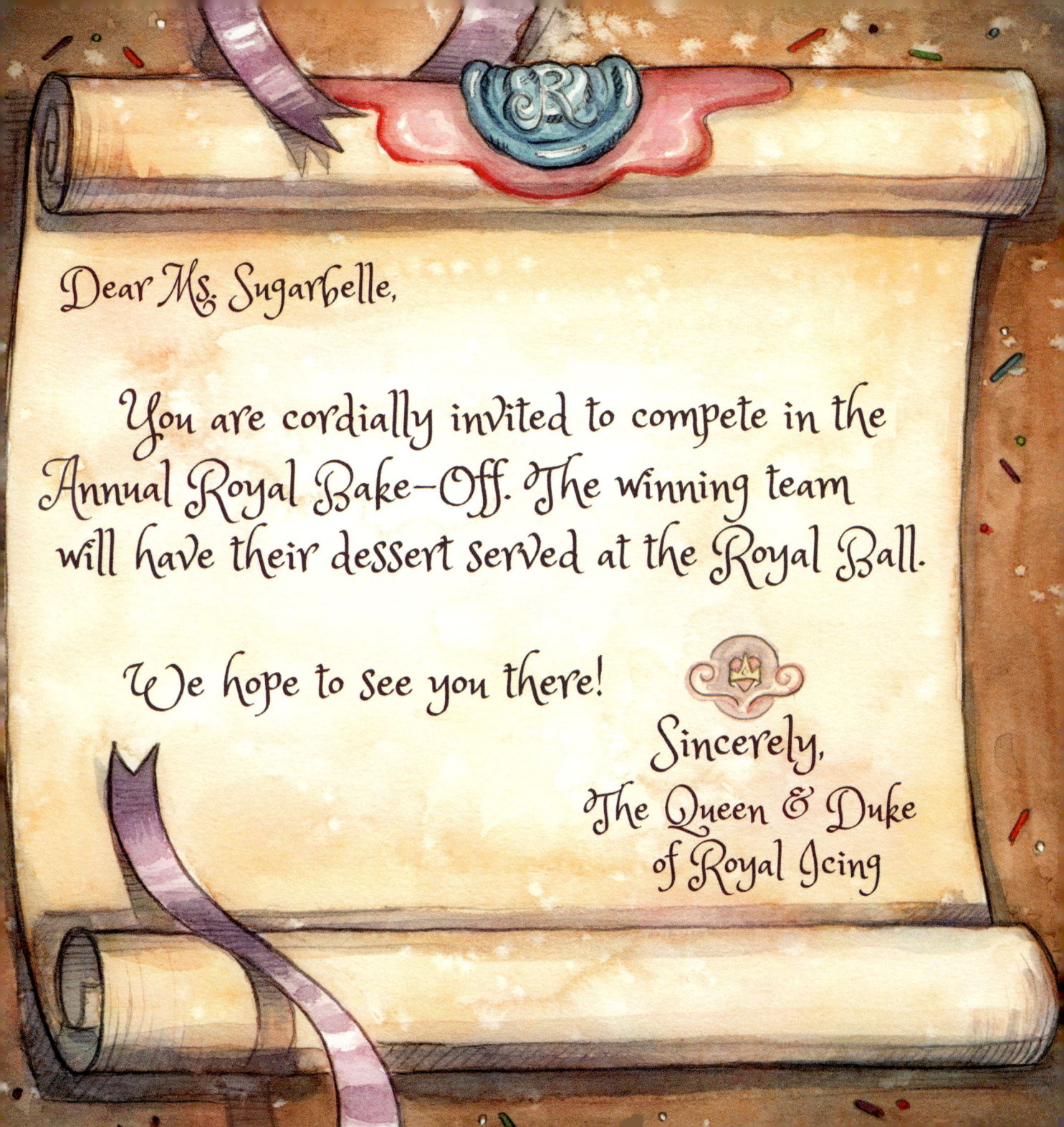

Sugarbelle, the Cookie Fairy, gulped as she arrived at the frosting-covered castle.

Her glittery wings fluttered as thousands of people from the town of Royal Icing lined the street, hoping to get a glimpse inside.

She began to relax as she noticed her friends Princess Mocha and Princess Cinnamon entering the castle.

"I can't believe we might have our cookies featured at the Royal Ball, Lemmy!" she said, squishing her loyal companion's furry face.

"Come on, Lemmy. Let's go inside. We got this!"

"Bakers! Welcome to the Palace of Royal Icing," announced the kitchen director, Chocolate Chip.

"Please gather 'round so I can introduce you to this year's panel of judges."

"Avocado? How in the world do we add avocado to cookies, Lemmy?" Sugarbelle whispered. He put his chocolate chip cookie paws on her hands.

"BAKERS, ARE YOU READY?" yelled Chocolate Chip.

Suddenly, the kitchen door slammed open and in walked the Red Velvet Queen and her evil minion, Mr. Fudge.

"So sorry to be tardy to the party," said the Red Velvet Queen, whipping her cape at the contestants.

Queen Almond graciously stood up.

"I'm sorry, dear sister, but I'm afraid you're too late."

"Oh, I'm sure there is room for one more team. Besides, everyone loves my red velvet cookies." The kitchen fell silent. Queen Almond dismissed her sister with her hand and allowed her to enter.

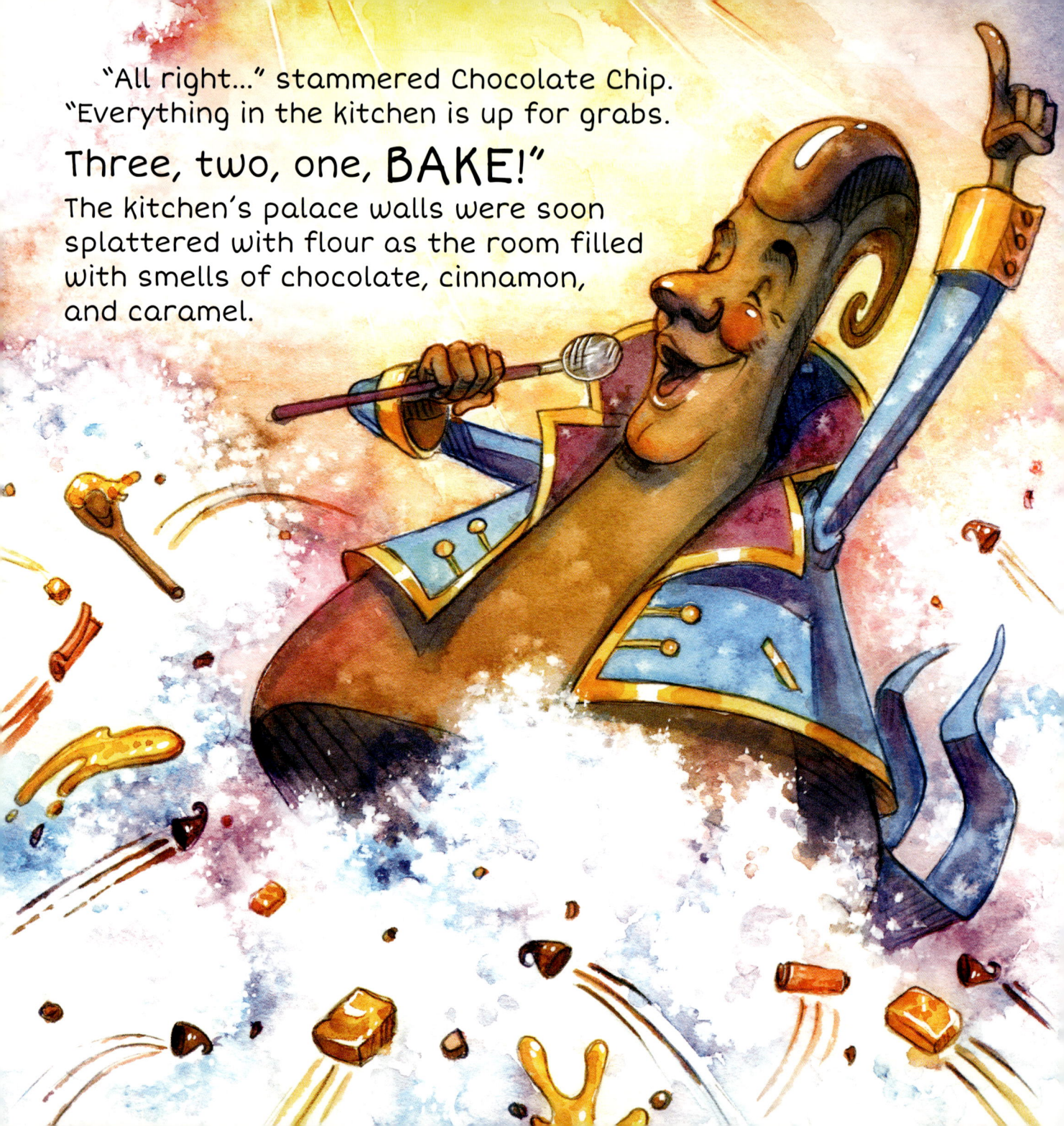

"All right..." stammered Chocolate Chip. "Everything in the kitchen is up for grabs.

Three, two, one, BAKE!"

The kitchen's palace walls were soon splattered with flour as the room filled with smells of chocolate, cinnamon, and caramel.

Sugarbelle and Lemmy prepped their station for their famous chocolate chip cookies.

"Okay, boy. Go fetch the flour, salt, and avocados. I'll grab the chocolate since you can't eat that."

Lemmy wagged his tail and trotted off to the pantry.

"Oh, how deliciously evil you are, my Queen." They both cackled quietly amongst themselves.

Lemmy raced back to Sugarbelle and tugged on her apron.

"HEY! My oven was turned up. My cookies are burnt!" yelled a contestant.

The Red Velvet Queen tiptoed away.

Lemmy let out a low growl.

"Oh no!" shouted another contestant. "My mixer has broken... our cookies are ruined!"

Mr. Fudge snickered, running away.

"And how, um…" Chocolate Chip began.

"How is team Princess Mocha and Princess Cinnamon doing?" he asked, noting the flour everywhere.

"Ohh!" Princess Mocha whirled around with chocolate all over her face.

"We will get this mess taken care of! Our cookies will be worth it in the end!" Princess Cinnamon beamed.

"We can't wait to try them!" Chocolate Chip said, smacking his lips.

Sugarbelle was just adding the finishing touches to her own cookies when she saw Mr. Fudge grab Lemmy from underneath the Red Velvet Queen's table.

"That's simply not true!" Sugarbelle cried.

"I think they should be disqualified, don't you?" stated the Red Velvet Queen.

"Right away!" stuttered Chocolate Chip. "I'm sorry, Ms. Sugarbelle, but you and Lemmy have been disqualified. Please go and clean your station."

Mr. Fudge was just about to add expired chocolate into a baker's cookies when Lemmy dashed across the kitchen and tugged on his apron.

Cookies flew high in the air and rained down on the judges.

"That's enough!" Queen Almond announced. "Ms. Sugarbelle, can you please explain what's going on here?"

"Well, Your Majesty, Mr. Fudge and the Red Velvet Queen have been messing with the baker's desserts and equipment. If Lemmy hadn't stopped Mr. Fudge, more cookies would be destroyed."

Queen Almond sighed.

"I'm so sorry, everyone. It is my fault for always trying to see the good in her. Sugarbelle and Lemmy, I do apologize for disqualifying you, but unfortunately, I'm afraid your cookies cannot be presented."

"Are there any bakers left whose cookies haven't been tampered with?"

A few contestants, including Princess Mocha and Princess Cinnamon, raised their hands.

"Please come forward for judgement."

"Princess Mocha and Princess Cinnamon!"

Sugarbelle hugged her friends and congratulated them.

"We look forward to eating your cookies at the Royal Ball," said Queen Almond.

"Your Majesty?" asked Princess Mocha and Princess Cinnamon. "We were wondering if everyone here could attend the Royal Ball as our guests, for all their baking efforts?"

"I think that is a wonderful idea, girls!"

The kitchen burst into cheers!

"Perhaps we could attend the Ball together?"

Lemmy licked the prince's face.

"And Lemmy, too!"

"We'd be delighted!" said Sugarbelle.

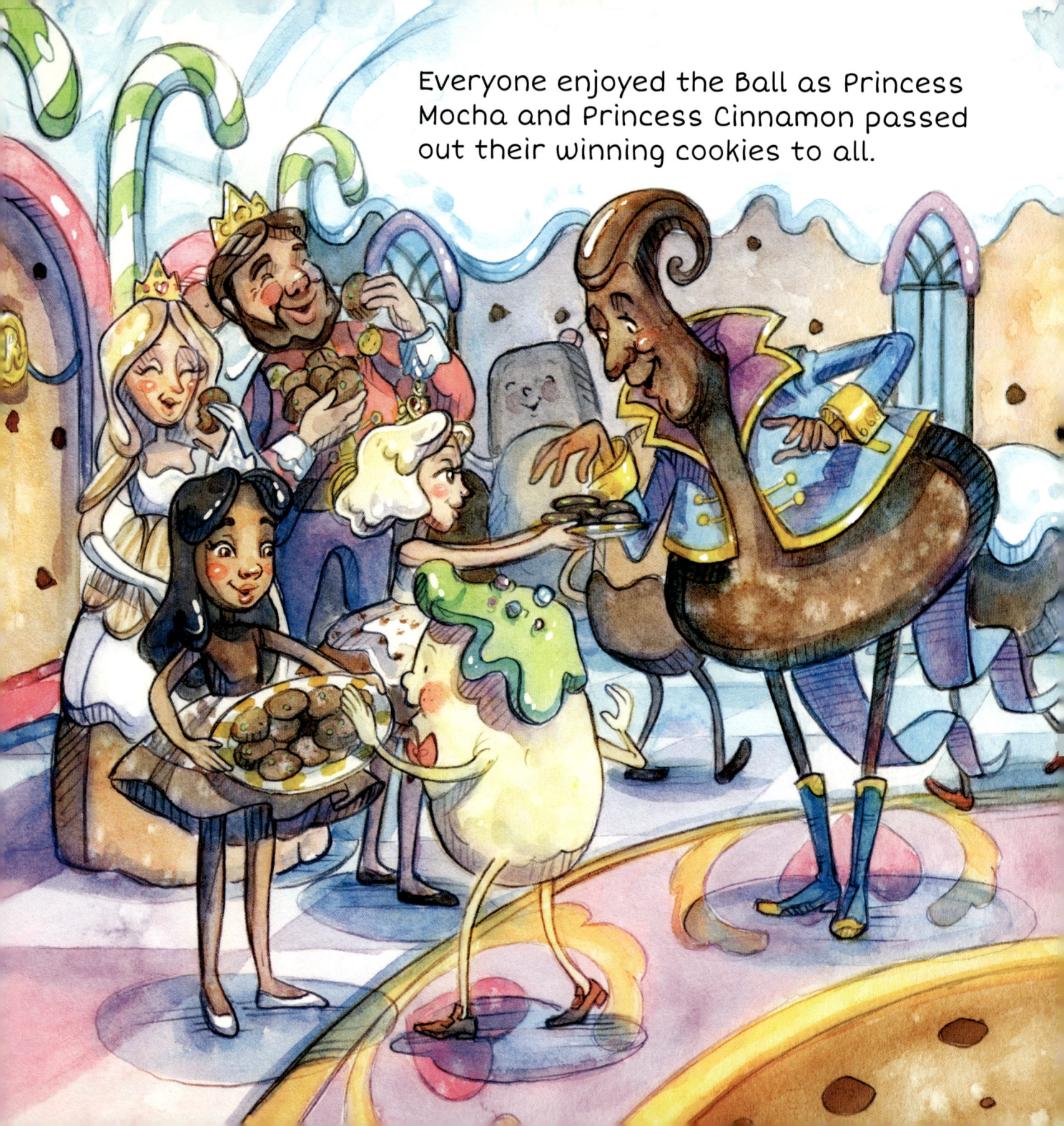

Everyone enjoyed the Ball as Princess Mocha and Princess Cinnamon passed out their winning cookies to all.

Thank you for all your love and support throughout the years!

Love,
MGC